CONSECUTION

Tayler Carter

13HORROR.COM BOOKS
An imprint of
DIZZY EMU PUBLISHING
1714 N McCadden Place, Hollywood, Los Angeles 90028
www.dizzyemupublishing.com

Consecution
Tayler Carter

ISBN: 9798790954542

First published in the United States
in 2021 by 13Horror.com Books/Dizzy Emu Publishing

1 3 5 7 9 10 8 6 4 2

CONSECUTION

Tayler Carter

Story by
Tayler Carter and Peter Gienke

INT. CATHOLIC CHURCH - DAY

Organ music plays as the MEMBERS OF THE CHURCH shuffle out.

FATHER JOHN shakes hands with the last person as they exit.
He closes the door behind them and enters the main section of
the church. It is silent.

Sitting alone in one of the pews is a MYSTERIOUS MAN. Father
John stops.

                    FATHER JOHN
          Excuse me, service has ended. I'm
          afraid we've got to close up.

The man doesn't move.

                    FATHER JOHN (CONT'D)
          Hello?

Father John walks over to the man who remains still. He
places his hand on the man's shoulder.

The man is wearing a white collared shirt with a single red
spot on his shoulder. Around his neck is a cross necklace.

                    MYSTERIOUS MAN
          I need to confess.

                    FATHER JOHN
          Confessions happen before mass. I
          would be more than happy to sit
          down with you next week if you stop
          by then.

                    MYSTERIOUS MAN
          I need to confess, Father John.

Father John narrows his eyes.

                    FATHER JOHN
          I'm sorry, but I don't think I know
          your name...

Silence. Father John doesn't press it.

                    FATHER JOHN (CONT'D)
          Very well, follow me to the
          confessional.

Father John signals the man to follow.

INT. CONFESSIONAL - MOMENTS LATER

Father John opens the door for one side of the booth and
signals for the man to enter. The man remains still, fists
clenched.

                    FATHER JOHN
          Go ahead, son. After you.

The man enters the booth and Father John enters through the
other side of the Grille. He sits in a chair facing away from
the man.

                    FATHER JOHN (CONT'D)
          Please feel free to take a seat.

The man doesn't move.

                    FATHER JOHN (CONT'D)
          May I have your name so that-

                    MYSTERIOUS MAN
          Father, bless me for I have sinned.

                    FATHER JOHN
          Okay, we'll skip that part. Please
          tell me son, what brings you here
          today?

                    MYSTERIOUS MAN
          I've committed evil deeds that I
          believe are irredeemable.

                    FATHER JOHN
          Nonsense, nothing is irredeemable,
          my child. Tell me what you have
          done that is so wrong and we can
          work through this together.

                    MYSTERIOUS MAN
          Do you believe in free will,
          Father?

                    FATHER JOHN
          I'm sorry?

                    MYSTERIOUS MAN
          Do you believe that we are the ones
          who choose how our lives end up?

                    FATHER JOHN
          The Bible states that free will is
          granted to every man.
                    (MORE)

                    FATHER JOHN (CONT'D)
          If he desires to incline towards
          the good and righteous, he has the
          power to do so; and if he desires
          to incline towards the unrighteous
          and evil, he also has the power to
          do so. Why do you ask such
          philosophical questions?

                    MYSTERIOUS MAN
          My wife...

                    FATHER JOHN
          Go on.

                    MYSTERIOUS MAN
          And the others...

                    FATHER JOHN
          Others?

                    MYSTERIOUS MAN
          Three total.

                    FATHER JOHN
          I'm not sure if I follow.

                    MYSTERIOUS MAN
          I killed them, all of them.

                    FATHER JOHN
          You-...

Father John's eyes fill with horror.

                    MYSTERIOUS MAN
          With my bare hands.

The man lifts up his hands. Father John sits up in his seat.

                    FATHER JOHN
          My dear child, why would you do
          such a thing?

                    MYSTERIOUS MAN
          They told me I had to...

                    FATHER JOHN
          Who's they?

                    MYSTERIOUS MAN
          They told me I must kill all four
          and then I will be free.

                    FATHER JOHN
          Four? But- Please, help me
          understand.

Nothing.

Father John turns around to see the man silently staring
straight ahead.

                    MYSTERIOUS MAN
          Father John, you call yourself a
          man of God, but we both know that
          your past says otherwise.

                    FATHER JOHN
          I'm afraid I don't know what you're
          talking about.

                    MYSTERIOUS MAN
          Do you have something to confess?

                    FATHER JOHN
          I try to live my life as a Godly
          figure for myself, my family, and
          my neighbors. I never intend to
          stray, though no one is perfect-

                    MYSTERIOUS MAN
          -You don't remember me, do you? I
          could tell in your eyes that you've
          forgotten my face, but I haven't
          forgotten yours.

                    FATHER JOHN
          Have we met?

The man grasps his necklace.

                    MYSTERIOUS MAN
          The altar hasn't changed but has
          the face of the boy whose innocence
          was taken.

Father John lets out a gasp.

                    FATHER JOHN
          Jimmy?

The man turns his gaze to Father John. His eyes are glowing
grey. He smirks.

                    MYSTERIOUS MAN
          Hello, Father.

5.

LATER

A bloody trail of footsteps leads to Jimmy standing at the alter. His white shirt now covered in Father John's blood.

He holds the cross necklace in his hand. It too is covered in blood. He stands unnerved.

                    VOICE (O.C.)
          At last, the process has been
          complete! Hail the Process!

                    GROUP OF VOICES (O.C.)
          Hail the Process!

Wide of the Church.

BLACK.

                    MALCOLM (V.O.)
          Most people think that war is about
          killing your adversaries. However,
          you can read as much military
          doctrine as you wish. The word,
          "kill" is never used in training
          Soldiers. Soldiers are trained to
          shoot, move, and communicate.
          Trained to neutralize the threat.
          Once I got out, I struggled to
          separate that psychological
          perception of war from my personal
          life. I guess that's why I'm
          here...

TITLE:

          1942

T.V. SCREEN -- DAY

The screen is black for a moment before a Black and White commercial comes on.

                    MALCOLM (O.C.)
          It's starting!

                    MIA (O.C.)
          Hold on, I'm fixing my hair.

                    MALCOLM (O.C.)
          Fix it in here!

                    MIA (O.C.)
          I'm almost done!

A box of *JOHNSON LITE* beer sits on the shelf in a fridge. A
WOMAN'S HAND grabs it.

INT. LIVING ROOM - DAY

A GROUP OF FRIENDS sit around a table playing cards. The
woman sets the box on the table and they all grab a beer.

                    MALCOLM (O.C.)
          Look, look! There I am! Mia, come
          in here!

                    ANNOUNCER (V.O.)
          Having a game night with friends?
          Try a cool, refreshing *Johnson
          Lite*. Guaranteed to have a good
          time!

Malcolm's character knocks his beverage with another extra's.

                    MIA (O.C.)
          Coming!

Footsteps stumble into the room.

INT. MALCOLM'S TRAILER - LIVING ROOM - DAY

MIA is using a curling iron on her hair. She is in nurse's
attire. Malcolm sits slouched on the couch, *Johnson Lite* in
hand.

The trailer is small, claustrophobic. Dirty clothes cover
every inch of the floor and last week's leftovers sit on the
stove. Hanging from the walls are full-size movie posters.

                    MALCOLM
          Well it's over now, so you can go
          back to what you were doing.

                    MIA
          I'm sorry, I've gotta get ready for
          work.

                    MALCOLM
          Okay.

Malcolm returns his gaze to the T.V.

Mia begins to walk back to the bathroom at the end of the
hall. She stops as she passes the kitchen. There are
envelopes of mail sitting at the edge of the counter.

Mia picks up the envelopes and fingers through them.

                    MIA
          You seriously need to take care of
          these bills today.

Malcolm waves his hand at Mia, signaling her to leave.

                    MIA (CONT'D)
          I mean it, I'm tired of bathing in
          cold water.

                    MALCOLM
          Yeah, yeah.

Mia stops on an envelope. She eyes the back of Malcolm's
head.

                    MIA
          Have you looked through these yet?

                    MALCOLM
          Bunch of bills. Bunch of ads.

                    MIA
          This one says it's from the U.S.
          Government and requires immediate
          action.

                    MALCOLM
          What's that?

Malcolm turns to Mia. She hands him the envelope. He opens it
and reads the letter inside.

His expression changes to horror. The heading reads: *"NOTICE
OF DRAFT"*.

                    MIA
          What's wrong?

                    MALCOLM
          I've been drafted...

Silence.

Malcolm brushes his hair back. Mia places her hand on his
shoulder.

                    MIA
          Are you going to be okay?

Malcolm takes a drink from his beverage and calmly sets it
down. For a moment, Malcolm appears to be taking the news
rather well.

Suddenly, he quickly jumps up from the couch. He makes a b-
line for the bathroom.

INT. BATHROOM - DAY

Malcolm pukes in the toilet. Mia stands above him, patting
his back.

                    MIA
          Do you need me to get you a glass
          of water?

He waves his hand at her and speaks into the toilet.

                    MALCOLM
          No, grab me a cigarette.

Mia squeezes Malcolm's arm and exits the bathroom. As he
pukes, she grabs her nurse hat from the sink counter and puts
it on.

INT. KITCHEN - DAY

Mia grabs a pack of cigarettes sitting next to the pile of
envelopes. A yellow envelope is sticking out from the rest,
it is addressed to her. She places it in her pocket.

INT. BATHROOM - DAY

Malcolm is back on his feet. He splashes water over his face
and looks in the mirror. Mia enters and hands him the
cigarettes.

He quickly snatches them from her hand and takes one out. He
places it in his mouth and searches his pockets for a
lighter.

Mia opens the bathroom mirror to reveal a medicine cabinet.
Sitting on a shelf is a lighter. Malcolm takes it off the
shelf and lights his cigarette. He takes a drag.

                    MALCOLM
          Who needs a weight loss program
          when you've got a draft letter?

He laughs at his own joke. An awkward silence. He steps
closer to Mia and runs his hand along her face.

                    MALCOLM (CONT'D)
          Let's get married.

                    MIA
          What?

                    MALCOLM
          Sure it's a little impulsive, but
          if we love each other, why the hell
          not?

                    MIA
          I just don't see how we can get our
          families together before you
          leave...

                    MALCOLM
          We can go down to the courthouse
          and have your sister and Ken as
          witnesses. This doesn't have to be
          some elaborate thing.

                    MIA
          I don't think they can legally
          accept my sister in her condition
          as a witness.

                    MALCOLM
          Look, if you don't want to marry
          me, just say it. You don't have to
          keep making excuses.

                    MIA
          It's not that. I just want to make
          sure we aren't rushing into
          something without being sure about
          it.

                    MALCOLM
          You're right. Two years is nothing.
          Who could possibly be sure about
          something after such a short period
          of time?

                    MIA
          That's not what I'm saying. I want
          to marry you-

                    MALCOLM
          -Then what's stopping you?

Mia grasps Malcolm's hand.

>   MIA
>   Make it back to me. Come back alive
>   and I'll be ready.

>   MALCOLM
>   I will. I promise.

EXT. TRAINING BASE - DAY

It's a rainy day. Malcolm is now dressed in military attire crawling through mud under barbed-wire. He gets caught on the wire. OTHER SOLDIERS crawl past him with ease.

He tugs his clothing, trying to free himself, to no avail. CHIEF, a large Native American, stops beside him and frees him. He then takes Malcolm's gun and carries it for him.

>   CHIEF
>   Keep up, Pretty Boy!

Chief continues to crawl through the mud, Malcolm stares on in disbelief before following.

Next, Malcolm clumsily climbs up a cargo net. Once at the top, he is unable to get himself over to the other side to go down.

Chief offers his hand and pulls Malcolm over the top and the two climb down the other side together.

Back on the ground, they run side-by-side.

>   CHIEF (CONT'D)
>   So what's your name? Or do you just
>   prefer to be called Pretty Boy?

Malcolm strains to get out a response between breaths.

>   MALCOLM
>   Malcolm.

>   CHIEF
>   Nice meeting you.

>   MALCOLM
>   Yours?

>   CHIEF
>   Lawrence, everyone just calls me
>   Chief.

INT. CHOW HALL - DAY

Chief and Malcolm sit at a table together. Malcolm brushes
some peas off of his meat.

                    CHIEF
          You got a job on the outside?

                    MALCOLM
          I'm an actor.

                    CHIEF
          Anything I've heard of?

                    MALCOLM
          Johnson Lite commercial?

                    CHIEF
          Big leagues, huh?

                    MALCOLM
          It's a start. Been trying for years
          to get into pictures.

                    CHIEF
          Well, you're a handsome man. It's
          only a matter of time.

INT. BATHROOM - DAY

The two are alone mopping the floor.

                    MALCOLM
          Got a wife?

                    CHIEF
          Yep, and two sons, Jack and Jeremy,
          twins.

                    MALCOLM
          I bet that's a handful.

                    CHIEF
          Wouldn't know, they were born the
          day after I was shipped off to
          basic. Killed me to miss it.

                    MALCOLM
          That's rough.

                    CHIEF
          It's not ideal; but once I return
          home I'm taking some time off to be
          with my new family.

                    MALCOLM
          That'll be nice. I've got a girl
          back home that I plan to marry once
          I return.

                    CHIEF
          I'll be waiting for the invitation
          in the mail.

INT. BARRACKS - NIGHT

Malcolm and Chief have beds next to each other. Malcolm is
holding something in his hand.

                    CHIEF
          What you got there?

                    MALCOLM
          Just a little piece of back home.

Chief sits back in his bed and takes a deep breath.

                    CHIEF
          That's good. Don't lose sight of
          what we're fighting for. A lot of
          good men end up losing their minds
          because they don't have anything to
          keep them in reality.

Chief points at Malcolm

                    CHIEF (CONT'D)
          Never forget who *you* are.

                    MALCOLM
          I don't think I'm ready...

                    CHIEF
          No one is ready to take another
          man's life. When it comes down to
          it, it's either us or them.

Malcolm lays down in his bed and pulls over his covers.

                    MALCOLM
          I suppose so.

He places the object under his pillow case. It's a picture of Mia. The DRILL SERGEANT enters the barracks.

                    DRILL SERGEANT
          Alright ladies, lights out!

He turns off the lights.

EXT. GERMAN WILDERNESS - NIGHT

At the edge of the tree line is a German bunker. A squad of SOLDIERS kneel silently in a circle. Among them are Malcolm and Chief.

MYERS returns to the group from the direction of the bunker.

                    MYERS
          Full bunker, backdoor exit. No sign
          of traps.

NELSON stands up.

                    NELSON
          This is an extraction. They
          outnumber us two to one, we don't
          want to dance with them. Cox and
          Hill will sneak up to the bunker
          and throw in the explosives. Then
          Myers, Butler, and Hughes will
          serve lead to any survivors. Pretty
          Boy and Chief will provide cover
          fire. Sparks, you're with me, we're
          going to their flanks. Got it?

                    SQUAD
          Yes, Sir!

In front of the bunker are three corpses of U.S. soldiers nailed to makeshift crosses. The corpses are covered in blood and missing body parts.

On them are signs that read, *"AUF WIEDERSEHEN"*.

Cox and Hill slowly crawl up to the bunker. They are closely followed by Myers, Butler, and Hughes. Malcolm and Chief hide back in the trees, guns in hand.

Cox and Hill begin preparing their explosives as they near the bunker.

As Hill crawls, he steps onto a mine. He gasps as he looks to Cox for help. Suddenly, the mine explodes, sending Hill into the air and his legs the opposite direction.

Screaming comes from the bunker as the Germans mount their
machine guns. Cox's explosive detonates in his hands,
knocking him to the ground.

He looks down in shock as there are only nubs where his hands
used to be.

The Germans begin to reign fire on Myers, Butler, and Hughes.
Blood and smoke fills the air as the three men fall to the
ground.

Nelson throws a frag into the bunker and Sparks follows his
lead.

Chief fires at the Germans in the bunker as Nelson and Sparks
continue to throw in explosives. Malcolm falls to the ground
behind his tree, crying.

Nelson waves them over.

                    NELSON
          Let's go!

                    CHIEF
               (To Malcolm)
          Come on!

Chief runs towards the bunker. He stops after a few paces to
provide cover fire for Nelson and Sparks then continues.

Malcolm continues to cry behind his tree. He watches as the
others enter the bunker. He closes his eyes and takes a deep
breath then follows.

INT. BUNKER - NIGHT

The other men are taking ammunition and weapons from the dead
German soldiers.

                    NELSON
          Keep moving, we need to push them.
          Our men are down there and they
          need our help!

The remainder of the squad regroups and they head down stairs
in the bunker to the next level. At the bottom of the stairs
is a closed door.

Nelson signals the men to stay back. He pulls out a grenade
and removes the pin. He kicks open the door and throws the
grenade in.

The grenade goes off and the squad files into the room. They open fire on the remaining soldiers. Once all the bullets are used the men go into hand-to-hand combat.

One German soldier attacks Malcolm with a combat knife. They fall to the ground, German soldier on top. The German uses their force to push the knife into Malcolm's chest.

Malcolm holds back as best he can, teeth clenched. He reaches into his pocket and pulls out a flare. He ignites the flare and stabs the German's eye with it.

The German drops the knife, screaming. He claws at his eye. Malcolm grabs the knife and lodges it into the German's throat. He stabs the soldier again.

The soldier continues to flail his limbs so Malcolm continues to stab him. Finally, the German goes limp. Malcolm stands up and backs away from the body, dropping the knife.

He becomes aware of his surroundings. They're in a sleeping quarter. Bunk beds line the walls. At the end of the room is a massive metal sliding door.

Nelson is kneeling over the last-living German soldier. He punches the soldier in the face, breaking his nose. The soldier holds his hands over his face to shield from anymore blows.

Nelson pushes his hands aside and continues to beat the man to death by bashing his face in. Once the job is done, he gets back to his feet and examines his hand.

                    NELSON (CONT'D)
          Fuck, I think I broke it.

Sparks pulls out some bandages.

                    SPARKS
          Need a bandage?

Nelson pushes them away.

                    NELSON
          Get those out of my face. The other
          platoon will be here soon with
          their medic.

Chief kneels down to Malcolm and hands him a canteen.

                    CHIEF
          Here, take some of this. You'll
          feel better.

Malcolm accepts the canteen with a shaky hand. He spills most of the water as he attempts to drink it.

Nelson knocks on the metal door.

                    NELSON
          They must be behind here. Help me
          get this thing open.

Chief pats Malcolm's shoulder and joins the others to help pry the door open. The three men get a grip on the door and begin to push. They grunt as they slowly open it.

Once the door is open, it reveals American soldiers bound and gagged, sitting in the center of the room.

                    SPARKS
          Finally.

Sparks takes a step into the room. The soldiers inside all fearfully grunt under their gags.

                    NELSON
          Sparks, no!

Sparks steps on a tripwire. This sets off explosives in the room that engulfs everything in dust and rumble.

Malcolm crawls through the clouded room, searching for his squad. He approaches a pile of rocks with an arm sticking out.

He grabs the arm and pulls with all of his strength. He flies backwards with the arm in his hand. It's been severed from its owner.

He quickly lets go of the arm and continues searching. He picks up a helmet and Chief's head falls out and rolls on the ground. He backs up against the wall, hyper-ventilating.

Suddenly, lights begin to shine down from the top of the staircase. They enter the room and one light shines directly in Malcolm's face.

                    MAN WITH FLASHLIGHT
          What happened here?

BLACK.

                    THERAPIST (V.O.)
          Were there any other survivors?

INT. THERAPIST OFFICE - DAY

Malcolm is laying on a couch staring at the ceiling, fingers
inter-locked. The THERAPIST sits in a chair by him and takes
notes.

Next to them, a bowl of raisins sits on a coffee table.
Sitting by the bowl are two cups of tea.

                    MALCOLM
          Not a single one. All that blood
          shed in vain.

The Therapist takes a moment to let Malcolm regain his
composure.

                    THERAPIST
          The horrors of war are a beast no
          man can prepare for. Now that we've
          covered the trigger event, tell me
          what happened when you arrived back
          home.

Malcolm sits upright.

                    MALCOLM
          Well, I wouldn't call it a warm
          welcome home party.

                    THERAPIST
          Please elaborate.

                                        BEGIN FLASHBACK:

EXT./INT. VARIOUS - DAY

FRONT DOOR

Malcolm is suited up in his military attire, full duffel bags
in hand. He opens his door to reveal...

TRAILER

An engagement ring lays on the kitchen counter. Malcolm steps
inside. The sound of a woman moaning is heard from behind the
closed bedroom door at the end of the hall.

Malcolm slowly creeps up to the door. He pauses for a moment,
opens the door and finds Mia in bed with another man.

END FLASHBACK.

INT. THERAPIST OFFICE - DAY

                    THERAPIST
          Oh my.

                    MALCOLM
          Needless to say, I wasn't too
          thrilled about that.

                                        BEGIN FLASHBACK:

EXT. MALCOLM'S FRONT DOOR - DAY

Mia is outside of the trailer yelling at Malcolm who stands
inside the door. The man is waiting in his car on the side of
the street.

Malcolm throws a bag full of Mia's clothes outside into the
front yard and slams his door shut.

END FLASHBACK.

                    THERAPIST
          So you traveled across the ocean to
          serve your country and-

                    MALCOLM
          -And my fiancé cheated on me and I
          have a newfound fear of fireworks.

Silence. Both Malcolm and the Therapist pick up their cups of
tea and take a long drink. Malcolm breaks the silence by
setting the cup down.

                    MALCOLM (CONT'D)
          But I got a medal.

                    THERAPIST
          Mr. Tracey, you've suffered
          tremendous loss in such a short
          period of time-

                    MALCOLM
          -If you're about to suggest I get a
          dog, I'm going to walk out of this
          office right now.

Malcolm takes a moment to think about it.

                    MALCOLM (CONT'D)
          Actually, that's not too bad of an
          idea. Get a Pug, name him
          Eisenhower.

The Therapist shakes his head in disbelief.

                    THERAPIST
          No, that's not what I'm about to
          suggest. I am going to write you a
          prescription for this new
          experimental anti-depressant.

He takes out a prescription book.

                    THERAPIST (CONT'D)
          Tell me, do you have any allergies?

                    MALCOLM
          I'm not sure if I've ever been
          tested but I haven't had any
          problems in the past.

                    THERAPIST
          Great. Now, before I prescribe you
          this medication I must inform you
          that it can have some serious side
          effects.

                    MALCOLM
          How serious are we talking?

                    THERAPIST
          Headaches, amnesia, internal
          bleeding, sore throat,
          hallucinations, more depression.
          The usual.

                    MALCOLM
          If you think it will help and I can
          still drink, I'm all for it.

                    THERAPIST
          Yes, you can still drink. Of
          course, like any medication, you'll
          want to avoid drinking while taking
          it.

                    MALCOLM
          I think I can handle that.

The Therapist stands up. Malcolm follows suit.

                    THERAPIST
          Well, Mr. Tracey, it's been a
          pleasure meeting with you this
          evening. Please give me a call if
          you have any further questions and
          I will see you next Friday.

                    MALCOLM
          Thank you for meeting with me.

                    THERAPIST
          Well of course, anything for you,
          Mr. Tracey.

The two shake hands and the Therapist tears off the receipt
and hands it to Malcolm.

INT. KITCHEN - DAY (BLACK AND WHITE)

IDA, dressed in 1950s housewife attire is preparing a hearty
breakfast. She is in her late 30s, playing the role of
Martha.

Malcolm pokes his head into the kitchen. He takes a big
whiff.

                    MALCOLM
          Well that smells mighty fine,
          Martha.

Ida smiles.

                    IDA
          Good morning, dear. I knew that
          today was the day of your big
          business deal and didn't want you
          going in on an empty stomach.

                    MALCOLM
          That sounds just dandy. I'll be at
          the table reading today's paper.

                    IDA
          Be there in a minute.

INT. DINING ROOM - DAY

Malcolm sits at the table reading the paper. He shakes his
head.

                    MALCOLM
          Unbelievable.

Ida enters carrying the plate of breakfast for Malcolm and sits it on the table in front of him. He sets the paper down and smiles.

                    MALCOLM (CONT'D)
          Thank you.

Ida places her hand on his shoulder. Malcolm's smile turns to a frown.

                    MALCOLM (CONT'D)
          Uh, sweet heart?

                    IDA
          Yes, dear?

                    MALCOLM
          Where's my coffee?

                    IDA
          Oh, goodness me. My mistake. I'll
          be right back with a cup.

                    MALCOLM
          Thank you.

MOMENTS LATER

Ida walks back in and hands Malcolm the cup of coffee. He smiles as he takes it from her.

                    MALCOLM
          Much better.

He takes a drink.

                    MALCOLM (CONT'D)
          I couldn't imagine going into this
          important business meeting without
          a fresh cup of my Stark's Classic
          Roast Original to keep my mind
          focused and on track for success.

Ida and Malcolm both smile at us.

CLOSEUP - PACKAGE OF STARK'S CLASSIC ROAST ORIGINAL

                    ADVERTISEMENT VOICE V.O.
          Stark's Classic Roast Original, a
          proud sponsor of hard-working
          American's everywhere.
                    (MORE)

                    ADVERTISEMENT VOICE V.O. (CONT'D)
          A cup of Stark's is a cup of love.
          Do you love your spouse?

END BLACK AND WHITE.

INT. COMMERCIAL SET - DAY

Malcolm and Ida are still in position, smiling at the T.V.
camera.

                    DIRECTOR (O.C.)
          Cut. Wrap.

The two immediately drop their smiles.

Malcolm holds out a hand for Ida to shake.

                    MALCOLM
          Hey, great job.

Ida shakes her head.

                    IDA
          No, thank you.

She walks away. Malcolm follows.

                    MALCOLM
          What's that supposed to mean?

                    IDA
          Stop following me.

                    MALCOLM
          Not until you tell me what your
          deal is.

                    IDA
          My *deal* is that I know your kind.
          Handsome and charismatic. You think
          the world owes you something.

                    MALCOLM
          I'm not some entitled prick. So if
          that's what you think, you're
          wrong. I was just trying to offer a
          friendly gesture.

Ida and Malcolm arrive at the bathrooms.

                    IDA
          Look, we're professionals, or at
          least we're supposed to be. I'm not
          going to be one of your conquests.
          I've been down that road and it
          never ends well.

Ida storms into the women's bathroom, slamming the door
behind her. Malcolm stands, bewildered.

                    MALCOLM
          Bitch.

Malcolm checks his watch and steps into the men's restroom.

INT. BATHROOM - NIGHT

Malcolm splashes water onto his face. He wipes off the water
with a handkerchief. He then reaches in his pocket and pulls
out a pill bottle.

                    MALCOLM
          Alright, do your magic.

Malcolm takes a pill. He then takes a deep breath and closes
his eyes. When he opens them, his reflection's eyes are still
closed for a brief moment before opening.

Malcolm catches this and narrows his eyes for a moment.

INT. CAR (MOVING) - NIGHT

As Malcolm drives, he checks his gas. It's nearly empty. He
pulls into a gas station.

EXT. GAS STATION - NIGHT

Malcolm finishes pumping his gas. He puts the pump back and
walks towards the gas station.

An EMPLOYEE is sweeping outside.

                    EMPLOYEE
          Be in there in a minute. Just
          finishing up out here.

INT. GAS STATION - NIGHT

Malcolm steps into the gas station. The lights are
flickering. He walks over to the counter and waits for the
employee.

Suddenly, the lights go out in the gas station. The man
outside is gone. Malcolm rushes to the door, locked. He bangs
on the window.

Then, a light flickers at the end of the aisle of snacks
Malcolm is standing next to. Illuminated under the light is
the metal sliding door from the German bunker.

Malcolm stands, frozen in fear. A loud pounding sound comes
from the door. Again and again it repeats.

Without realizing it, Malcolm has moved closer to the door.
He now stands only a few feet away from it.

Silence.

The door quickly slides open with a roar. It produces a
strong gust of wind that knocks Malcolm off his feet.

Nothing is visible behind the door except darkness. The sound
of something slimy can be heard from behind the door. Slowly,
a head rolls out from behind it.

It keeps rolling until it stops directly in front of Malcolm.
It's Chief! Malcolm hastily shuffles back against a wall. A
voice whispers from the darkness behind the door.

                    MYSTERIOUS VOICE
          Malcolm.

A grey, decrepit hand slowly emerges out of the darkness and
silently signals Malcolm to come closer.

Malcolm gets to his feet. Something grabs him from behind. He
jumps as he turns around.

                    EMPLOYEE
          I'm sorry. Didn't mean to startle
          you.

Malcolm is panting heavily. The lights in the Gas Station are
back on and the metal door gone.

INT. TRAILER - NIGHT

Malcolm enters through the front door and immediately a SMALL
PUG runs up, desperate to meet him. He bends down to happily
receive the dog.

                    MALCOLM
          Hey buddy. Sorry I'm late.

Malcolm tries to take a step forward but the pug runs in
front of him and jumps up and down his legs.

                    MALCOLM (CONT'D)
          Hold on a sec, I just got back.

The pug stops jumping and walks to the front door.

                    MALCOLM (CONT'D)
          Let me put my things down first.

It sits in place, staring up at Malcolm with beady eyes.

                    MALCOLM (CONT'D)
          Alright, I'm coming. Don't give me
          that shit.

EXT. TRAILER PARK - NIGHT

Malcolm walks the dog to a small fenced-in dog park. He sits
on a bench while the pug does his business.

                    MALCOLM
          Hurry up, Eisenhower. We don't want
          to miss the movie.

Most of the lights are out in the trailer park. The night
breeze fills the air, accompanied by the sounds of crickets
chirping and Eisenhower's panting.

In the far distance is a man standing in a white robe. The
man appears to be watching Malcolm. Malcolm squints his eyes
to get a better look.

Eisenhower snarls in the direction of the man. This causes
Malcolm to tense with fear. He looks to the dog for a moment,
then back up where the man was standing but now he is gone.

He holds his gaze for a moment longer.

INT. TRAILER - NIGHT

Malcolm enters and Eisenhower rushes to the couch.

                    MALCOLM
          I'll be there in a minute, big guy.

INT. KITCHEN - NIGHT

Malcolm grabs an entire six pack of *Johnson Lite* from the
fridge.

He then fills Eisenhower's food bowl.

                    MALCOLM
          Dinner's on the table!

Eisenhower storms in and heads to the bowl.

INT. LIVING ROOM - NIGHT

Malcolm sits on the couch and sets the six pack on the coffee
table. Eisenhower comes in after him and jumps back up next
to him.

                    MALCOLM
          Movie time!

Eisenhower barks at Malcolm. Malcolm appears to get offended
by what Eisenhower just said.

                    MALCOLM (CONT'D)
          No, I'm not going to get scared. If
          I recall correctly, that was you
          who was hiding under the cushions
          last time.

Eisenhower barks again.

                    MALCOLM (CONT'D)
          Well, you and I remember things
          very differently.

Malcolm cracks open a beer and signals for Eisenhower to be
quiet.

                    MALCOLM (CONT'D)
          Alright, alright. It's about to
          start.

The commercial ends and the movie title comes up: *"The
Devil's Disciples"*.

                    MALCOLM (CONT'D)
          Haven't seen this one yet.
                  (To Eisenhower)
          You know, I saw Tony Jacobson at-

Eisenhower growls at Malcolm.

                    MALCOLM (CONT'D)
          Sorry.

Eisenhower lays down on the couch, facing the T.V. Malcolm
sits back comfortably to watch the movie.

LATER

All six beer cans sit on the table, empty. The *National
Anthem* plays on the Television as Malcolm sits on the couch,
head back, mouth open, snoring. Eisenhower lays, sleeping in
his lap.

INT. TRAILER - LIVING ROOM - DAY

The phone rings. This wakes Malcolm with a start, who is
still sleeping on the couch.

He lazily staggers to the kitchen.

INT. KITCHEN -DAY

Yawning, he takes the phone off of the receiver on the wall.

                    MALCOLM
          Malcolm speaking.

INT. OFFICE - DAY

KEN is resting his feet on his desk. Papers scattered
everywhere. He has a receding hairline, wears glasses,
slight.

                    KEN
          Hey, Malcolm.

INTERCUT

                    MALCOLM
          Ken! My man! How are things going?

                    KEN
          I've got some good news for you--
          no, great news!

                    MALCOLM
          Well, let's hear it.

                    KEN
          I just got off the phone with
          Lumière Pictures. They want you!

                    MALCOLM
          They want *me*?

                    KEN
          That's right.

                    MALCOLM
          And you're sure they said my name?

                    KEN
          Yes, they want Malcolm Tracey to
          star in a role in an upcoming film.

                    MALCOLM
          Ken, you wonderful son of a bitch!
          If you were here I'd kiss you!

                    KEN
          I would really rather you didn't.

                    MALCOLM
          What's the film?

                    KEN
          They're not able to give that out
          yet, but I was told to inform you
          that the director wants to meet
          with you next week.

                    MALCOLM
          Mia always said I'd never get
          anywhere with you as my agent, but
          look at me now!

                    KEN
          She said that?

                    MALCOLM
          Let me grab a notepad.

Malcolm looks at the clock on his oven.

                    MALCOLM (CONT'D)
          Shit, my appointment!

                    KEN
          What?

                    MALCOLM
          Look, I've got to go. We'll talk
          later.

                    KEN
          Okay, just-

Malcolm hangs up the phone.

INT. BEDROOM - DAY

Malcolm digs through his closet. Articles of clothing cover
the entire floor. He picks up a shirt and reveals a worn-down
box sitting on the closet floor.

He pauses for a moment then kneels down to the box. He opens
the flaps and inside lays his folded uniform from his time in
the service.

He takes the uniform out and sets it aside. Underneath it are
the canteen that Chief gave him, the knife from the soldier
he killed, and a medal.

He picks up the jug to examine it. He then gently places it
back in the box and glances at the knife for a moment. His
reflection stares back at him in the blade.

Malcolm puts the uniform back in the box and closes it.

INT. THERAPIST OFFICE - DAY

The Therapist is reading a small yellow book as he sits in
his chair waiting for Malcolm. While he reads, he eats
handfuls of raisins.

A bell rings. Malcolm enters through the front door of his
office. The Therapist closes the book and stands up to greet
Malcolm, smiling.

                    THERAPIST
          Mr. Tracey, good morning.

                    MALCOLM
          Sorry I'm late.

The Therapist waves his hand.

                    THERAPIST
          Oh, don't worry about it.

He offers the bowl of raisins to Malcolm. Malcolm rejects the
offer.

                    THERAPIST (CONT'D)
          Please, take a seat, get
          comfortable.

The Therapist gestures the couch. Malcolm takes a seat and
the Therapist sits across from him. He takes out a notebook
and a pen.

                    THERAPIST (CONT'D)
          So tell me about your week.

                    MALCOLM
          The treatment seems to be going
          well. Though, I've had some unusual
          experiences.

The Therapist takes notes while Malcolm talks.

                    THERAPIST
          Go on.

                    MALCOLM
          You said that hallucinations are a
          side-effect of the medication.

                    THERAPIST
          It's not an uncommon occurrence. As
          I stated when I prescribed you this
          medication, it's still in the
          experimental phase. The
          hallucinations should subside once
          your body becomes acclimated to the
          drug.

                    MALCOLM
          How long are we talking? Days,
          weeks?

                    THERAPIST
          There's no telling as it affects
          each patient differently. It has
          already proven to treat patients
          better than anything currently on
          the market. However, I understand
          if you wish to stop taking this
          because of your uncertainty.

                    MALCOLM
          No, I didn't mean that. I guess
          it's just not what I expected.

The Therapist smirks.

                    THERAPIST
          That's quite understandable. Before
          we go on, I failed to mention last
          time that there is actually a
          monthly conference held at a
          community center nearby. The
          purpose of this conference is for
          the creators to communicate
          information to the individuals,
          such as yourself, chosen to take
          this medication. I suggest checking
          this out if you're interested.

                    MALCOLM
          Yeah, I think that would be a good
          idea.

                    THERAPIST
          Excellent, let me write down the
          address for you.

The Therapist writes on the back of his business card and
hands it to Malcolm.

INT. COMMUNITY CENTER - NIGHT

Malcolm walks down a hall of doors. In front of one of them
is a sign that reads: *"Monthly Q&A"*. He enters.

INT. CONFERENCE ROOM - NIGHT

The walls of the room are painted yellow. In the center are
tables in the formation of a square sitting on top of a large
rug with a depiction of the Sun.

The room is full of strangers engaged in their own
conversations.

In the back, on a table, are drinks and snacks. Malcolm goes
to the table and grabs a glass of wine.

Next to the table is a globe. On the globe there are several
yellow pins marking various countries. Malcolm notices there
is a pin in Germany.

A doctor approaches and extends a hand.

                    DR. HERNANDEZ
          Dr. Hernandez.

Malcolm shakes his hand.

                    MALCOLM
          Malcolm.

                    DR. HERNANDEZ
          I don't think I've seen you here
          before.

                    MALCOLM
          First time.

                    DR. HERNANDEZ
          Wonderful! Welcome to our
          conference. I see you've found the
          wine.

Malcolm gestures at the globe.

                    MALCOLM
          What are the pins for?

                    DR. HERNANDEZ
          Oh, they're for, uh...

Almost as if on queue, another doctor joins in on the
conversation.

                    DR. SILVIA
          Dr. Hernandez.

                    DR. HERNANDEZ
          Dr. Silvia! Good to see you!

Dr. Hernandez grabs Malcolm's shoulder.

                    DR. HERNANDEZ (CONT'D)
          I was just chatting with our newest
          member here, Malcolm.

Malcolm shakes hands with Dr. Silvia.

                    DR. SILVIA
          It's a pleasure meeting you.

                    MALCOLM
          Likewise.

Dr. Silvia gestures to a larger group of doctors standing
nearby.

                    DR. SILVIA
          Allow me to introduce you to the
          others. Gentlemen, this is Malcolm.
          It's his first time here.

They all raise a glass to Malcolm.

                    DR. SILVIA (CONT'D)
          This is Dr. Gomez, Dr. Torres, Dr.
          Rubio, and Dr. Luis.

Malcolm forces a smile.

                    DR. SILVIA (CONT'D)
          Now that introductions are in
          order. Let's say we get started.

Dr. Silvia claps his hands. In an orderly fashion, all of the
attendees find a seat and sit down at the exact same time.
Malcolm follows suit.

Once seated, Dr. Hernandez begins.

                    DR. HERNANDEZ
          Good evening, gentlemen. Let's
          begin with our affirmations.

In unison, everyone in the room except Malcolm begins to
chant.

                    EVERYONE
          I am the architect of my life; I
          build its foundation and choose its
          contents.// My body is healthy; my
          mind is brilliant; my soul is
          tranquil.// My future is an ideal
          projection of what I envision
          now.// My efforts are being
          supported by the universe; my
          dreams manifest into reality before
          my eyes.// I am at peace with all
          that has happened, is happening,
          and will happen.// My life is just
          beginning.

The doctors all take out yellow leather-bound books.

                    DR. HERNANDEZ
          Before we get into the meat of
          tonight's discussion, do any of the
          doctors have a weekly they would
          like to share?

Dr. Torres stands up and everyone's eyes silently follow him.

                    DR. TORRES
          I have began treatment with a new
          prospect.

                    DR. HERNANDEZ
          How did they react to the
          prescription?

                    DR. TORRES
          They're taking it well. The Sun
          rises over another decade.

The doctors knock on their books to cheer.

                    EVERYONE
          Hail The Process!

                    DR. HERNANDEZ
          Very good. Anyone else?

Dr. Hernandez waits for a response, no one speaks up.

                    DR. HERNANDEZ (CONT'D)
          Very well. We have a new member
          joining us this evening.

The room fills with the sound of the doctors knocking on
their books.

                    DR. HERNANDEZ (CONT'D)
          For years now we have taken in
          special patients and put them
          through our unique treatment plan.

The doctors knock on their books.

                    EVERYONE
          Hail the Process!

                    DR. HERNANDEZ
          We have brothers and sisters across
          the globe currently implementing
          our treatment to great effect.

                    EVERYONE
          Hail the Process!

                    DR. HERNANDEZ
          And now we gather here today to
          discuss what makes this treatment
          so successful.

Malcolm raises his hand. Dr. Hernandez signals him to speak.

                    MALCOLM
          This medication has some serious
          side effects. I'm not sure if
          they're as prominent with other
          patients but I was wondering if I
          could get your thoughts on it.

The group erupts with disdain. Dr. Hernandez keeps his cool.

                    DR. HERNANDEZ
          Quiet! He is new to our
          organization, he doesn't know our
          customs yet.
                    (To Malcolm)
          Please forgive them, we haven't had
          a new member in quite some time.
                    (Back to the group)
          Now, Malcolm poses a great
          question. Any takers?

Dr. Torres stands up and addresses Malcolm.

                    DR. TORRES
          Between the six of us doctors there
          is a combined research of hundreds
          of years.

At this, Malcolm narrows his eyes in disbelief.

                    DR. TORRES (CONT'D)
          I understand your skepticism but
          believe me when I say that if you
          follow The Process, you'll unlock
          abilities that you've never dreamed
          of. It is a tried and true
          algorithm to cure any sickness and
          provide a long and prosperous life
          for anyone that follows it.

The doctors knock on their books.

                    EVERYONE
          Hail the Process!

                    MALCOLM
          I'm not familiar with this *Process*.
          I just came to learn more about the
          medication. If there's something
          more that needs to be done, please
          enlighten me.

                    DR. HERNANDEZ
          The Process is what guides us. It's
          the reason we are all here today.

The doctors knock on their books.

                    EVERYONE
          Hail the Process!

                    MALCOLM
          Yeah, well, forgive me but that
          doesn't really explain anything.

The doctors erupt in anger. Dr. Hernandez taps his wine glass
with a fork. The ringing silences everyone. They all freeze
in place except Malcolm.

As if planned ahead, the doctors all stand up in unison and
begin to chant in a different language. A darkness begins to
creep over the room.

                    DR. HERNANDEZ
          Do you submit your will to us and
          vow to adhere to The Process?

Malcolm blinks his eyes rapidly. The doctors slowly walk
towards him. He's surrounded. Their faces begin to warp into
inhuman shapes.

His vision becomes blurry.

                    DR. HERNANDEZ (CONT'D)
          Do you submit?

A wall of flames surrounds the group, encasing them in a
circle. Malcolm loses all life from his face, gaping.

This intense moment is broken by the shattering of a glass.
Blood trickles down Malcolm's hand. His wine glass that he
was holding lays on the table in pieces.

The room is silent. Malcolm falls to the ground unconscious.

BLACK.

INT. TRAILER - DAY

Malcolm awakes, Eisenhower in his lap. He is in his living
room on the couch. T.V. on. His hand is wrapped in a bandage.
He holds it up to inspect the bandage.

There is a knock at the door.

Malcolm gets up from the couch and checks the window.
Eisenhower walks over to the door and barks.

KNOCK KNOCK KNOCK...

Malcolm slowly inches towards the door.

KNOCK KNOCK KNOCK...

He places his hand on the door knob. He pauses for a moment, considering.

                    KEN
          I can see your car. I know you're
          in there.

Malcolm lets out a sigh and opens the door.

                    MALCOLM
          Hey.

                    KEN
          Someone looks like they woke up on
          the wrong side of the couch.

Eisenhower jumps up and down Ken's legs. Ken kneels down to pet him, bag of fast-food in hand.

                    KEN (CONT'D)
          Hey buddy. Better be taking care of
          your old man. He's got a big
          opportunity coming up.

                    MALCOLM
          I don't need to be taken care of.

                    KEN
          Thank God, I didn't want to share
          this food anyway.

Ken hugs the fast-food bag.

                    MALCOLM
          Did you get hash browns?

INT. LIVING ROOM - DAY

Malcolm and Ken are sitting in the living room eating breakfast.

                    KEN
          So you don't remember anything?

Malcolm lowers his bandaged hand below the table.

                    MALCOLM
          Nothing. Last thing I remember was
          everyone sitting down to begin to
          begin the meeting.

                    KEN
          You really need to stop taking this
          medication. It's messing with your
          mind. You won't be able to learn
          your lines.

                    MALCOLM
          My Therapist prescribed it. I trust
          him.

Ken takes a drink from his soda.

                    KEN
          Yeah, but you're constantly seeing
          visions and now you maybe have
          amnesia.

                    MALCOLM
          I wouldn't call it that.

                    KEN
          Then what would you call it?

                    MALCOLM
          I don't know.

                    KEN
          Well as your agent, I don't
          approve. But you know I can't stop
          you. Anyway, the meeting with the
          director.

                    MALCOLM
          Oh yeah, next weekend.

                    KEN
          That's right. He wants to meet with
          you at Sticky Big's. It'll be
          pretty informal. Just wants to get
          to know you to make sure you're fit
          for the part.

                    MALCOLM
          Great. I'll need to find someone to
          watch Eisenhower while I'm gone.

Malcolm takes a long drink from his soda, waiting for Ken to
speak up.

                    KEN
          Yeah, I'll watch the damn dog. Just
          ask next time.

                    MALCOLM
          Knew I could count on you.

                    KEN
          You owe me.

                    MALCOLM
          It's your job. I pay you to help.

                    KEN
          Yeah, well, win an Oscar or
          something, Jesus.

The two share a laugh.

INT. TRAILER - BATHROOM - NIGHT

Malcolm is behind the curtains taking a shower. He shuts the
water off, grabs a towel, and steps out. He opens the
medicine cabinet and takes out his pill bottle.

He swallows a pill and sets the open bottle on the sink.
Someone knocks on his front door. Still in his towel, Malcolm
exits the bathroom, leaving behind the open pill bottle.

INT. LIVING ROOM - NIGHT

Malcolm opens the door, it's Ken.

                    KEN
          I hope you're not going in that.

INT. MALCOLM'S CAR (MOVING) - NIGHT

Malcolm pulls into the parking lot for Sticky Big's. It's a
modest sized restaurant. Above it is a neon sign of a pig
holding a fork with a hotdog on the end.

Malcolm brushes his hair back. He checks his teeth in the
rearview mirror. As he does this, his reflection smirks back
at him.

He quickly turns the mirror away and slaps at his face.

                    MALCOLM
          Come on, not now. Hold it together.

Malcolm opens his glove compartment and pulls out a flask. He takes a swig and puts it away. Deep breath.

                    MALCOLM (CONT'D)
          Show time.

INT. STICKY BIG'S - NIGHT

Malcolm walks through the crowded restaurant. No sign of the director. It's a packed night, a live band plays blue grass in the back corner.

A hand raises and waves him over, it's QUENTIN HUSTON. He is wearing a Hawaiian shirt and khaki shorts. Malcolm walks over to the table and Quentin signals him to sit.

                    QUENTIN
          It's so good to finally meet you!

                    MALCOLM
          Likewise! Honestly, I can't believe
          this is actually happening right
          now.

                    QUENTIN
          Well I'm happy to tell you it is.

                    MALCOLM
          I'm a huge fan of your work. I have
          a *City Lights* poster in my living
          room.

                    QUENTIN
          Isn't that something? Tell me about
          yourself. Ken says you've been in
          the business for years now.

                    MALCOLM
          That's right! Well, maybe not quite
          your league. I've mostly done
          commercials and promos.

                    QUENTIN
          Hey, everyone's gotta start
          somewhere.

The WAITER arrives to their table.

                    WAITER
          Gentlemen. Are you ready to order?

Quentin waves his hand.

                    QUENTIN
          Not quite yet, we're waiting on one
          more.

Malcolm raises an eyebrow - *"Who could that be?"*.

                    QUENTIN (CONT'D)
          And there she is!

Malcolm turns around in his seat to find Ida walking towards
them.

                    IDA
          Hello!

Her expression drops as she notices Malcolm.

                    IDA (CONT'D)
          Oh...

Quentin signals her over.

                    QUENTIN
          Come, join us!

LATER

Ida and Quentin are sharing an enthusiastic exchange. Malcolm
sits, silent, three empty drinks in front of him.

                    QUENTIN
          It's unbelievable that something
          like that can happen by chance!

                    IDA
          I know!

                    QUENTIN
             (To Malcolm)
          So, as I understand, you two have
          worked together before. Tell me how
          that went.

                    MALCOLM
          Yeah, we did a commercial-

                    IDA
          Stark's Classic Roast Original.

                    QUENTIN
          Ah. Well, that's great that you've
          done work together. This doesn't
          normally happen.
                         (MORE)

                    QUENTIN (CONT'D)
          You two are definitely ahead of
          your competitors since you already
          have a grasp on each other's style.

                    IDA
          Absolutely.

                    MALCOLM
          Yeah.

                    QUENTIN
          I think we're good on the small
          talk for now. Let's go ahead and
          discuss the film.

                    IDA
          By all means.

Quentin leans in towards the table.

                    QUENTIN
          Now this is something that Malcolm
          actually has prior experience with.

Malcolm raises his eyebrows. Quentin smiles.

                    QUENTIN (CONT'D)
          I thought that would get your
          attention. We are shooting a *World
          War Two* film. A majority of the
          film will be set in Germany.

Quentin gestures the sky.

                    QUENTIN (CONT'D)
          The Fourth Unit - This is a
          courageous tale of the fourth wave
          of men sent undercover to take out
          a secret Nazi base where German
          physicians would perform
          experiments on prisoners of war.

                    MALCOLM
          That sounds like a neat premise.

                    QUENTIN
          They die.

                    MALCOLM
          Cheerful.

                    QUENTIN
          You two are the forbidden love
          story that acts as the centerpiece
          of the film. Malcolm as a member of
          the unit and Ida as the supervisor
          of the operation.

Ida gestures between Malcolm and herself.

                    IDA
          Oh, so we...

                    QUENTIN
          Mhm.

                    IDA
          Do we... Kiss?

                    QUENTIN
          What's a love story without a
          dramatic kiss?

                    IDA
          I just... Didn't realize it was
          that kind of story.

                    QUENTIN
          Well of course! You get two
          attractive people of the opposite
          sex together and sparks are sure to
          fly.

                    MALCOLM
          I'm assuming mouth wash will be on
          standby.

Quentin laughs.

                    QUENTIN
          You guys are too much! Really. Oh,
          I almost forgot! I have a special
          surprise.

Quentin picks up a briefcase from the floor and sets it on
the table. He opens it and pulls out two envelopes. He hands
one to Malcolm and the other to Ida.

                    IDA
          Oh, I love surprises!

Malcolm and Ida open their envelopes. They pull out plane
tickets.

                    MALCOLM
          Germany?

Quentin smiles.

                    IDA
          I've always wanted to go to
          Germany!

                    QUENTIN
          With a majority of our scenes
          taking place in Germany we actually
          found it more cost effective to
          shoot on location.

                    IDA
          This is so exciting! I have to tell
          my mother!

Malcolm has completely dissociated. His vision goes blurry
for a moment. When back in focus, he is now sitting alone in
a room. He is tied to his chair.

He struggles to get free but is trapped. The only exit is a
large doorway in front of him. He's back in the bunker.
Suddenly, the metal door slides shut and locks.

Fire engulfs the room around him and he can hear the doctors
chanting. The chanting gets louder and louder.

                    WAITER
          More water?

The waiter is standing over Malcolm. It is obvious this is
not the first time the waiter asked him this question as Ida
and Quentin are staring at him.

Malcolm waves his hand.

                    MALCOLM
          No, thank you.

Malcolm squeezes his plane ticket.

INT. MALCOLM'S CAR (MOVING) - NIGHT

Malcolm pulls his car into the driveway and notices a few
things that are strange: Ken's car is missing, the lights in
his trailer are on, and his front door is ajar.

He turns his car off. He holds his keys between his fingers
to use as a makeshift weapon and steps out of his car.

EXT. DRIVEWAY - NIGHT

Slowly, he creeps up to his front door.

INT. TRAILER - NIGHT

Malcolm quietly pushes the door, it creaks as it slowly
opens. He quietly steps inside and scans the room. Without
making a noise, he walks to his hallway.

The trailer is empty.

INT. KITCHEN - NIGHT

On the kitchen table is a note written by Ken.

*"Emergency trip to Beverly Hills Pet Hospital. Also,
Therapist called - meet at 6p.m. next Thursday at 132
Abuelita Ln."*

Malcolm opens one of the drawers in his kitchen and pulls out
a phone book. He searches in the B section and lands on
Beverly Hills Pet Hospital. He dials the number on his rotary
phone.

INT. PET HOSPITAL - FRONT DESK

                    DESK CLERK
          Good evening, thank you for calling
          Beverly Hills Pet Hospital, how may
          I help you?

INTER-CUT.

                    MALCOLM
          Hi, there is a man named Ken Ryan
          there with a small pug named
          Eisenhower. I need to speak with
          him.

                    DESK CLERK
          I'm sorry but guest information is
          confidential. I won't be able to do
          that. If you absolutely need to
          speak with him, feel free to stop
          by, we are open for another thirty
          minutes.

                    MALCOLM
          Listen lady, I'm an actor and that
          man is my agent, Ken, and he has my
          dog. Now you're going to do what I
          tell you to and put him on the
          line.

                    DESK CLERK
          Well by all means, sir. Allow me to
          accommodate you.

                    MALCOLM
          Thank you.

                    DESK CLERK
          Office hours are 8a.m. to 10p.m.

Dial tone. Malcolm slams his phone on the receiver. He clears
his throat then redials the Pet Hospital.

                    DESK CLERK (CONT'D)
          Good evening, thank you for calling
          Beverly Hills Pet Hospital, how may
          I help you?

This time, Malcolm takes a more relaxed approach.

                    MALCOLM
          Hello, this is Malcolm, we just
          spoke.

                    DESK CLERK
          Ah, the actor. I recall.

                    MALCOLM
          Listen, I apologize for the way I
          just acted, I may have been a
          little brash.

                    DESK CLERK
          Brash?

                    MALCOLM
          Okay, I was an asshole. I said that
          I'm sorry. Please, I need to know
          what condition my dog is in. Just
          let me speak with Ken.

The Desk Clerk lets out a sigh.

                    DESK CLERK
          One second.

                    MALCOLM
          Okay.

A moment passes as Malcolm waits in silence. He nervously
taps his foot in anticipation.

                    KEN
          Malcolm?

                    MALCOLM
          Ken! What's going on?

                    KEN
          I was just watching the tube and
          Eisenhower went M.I.A., next thing
          I knew, he was throwing up. I
          figured he would stop but he never
          did. So I decided I should take him
          to the Pet Hospital. But don't
          worry, he's fine now.

                    MALCOLM
          How could you let this happen?

                    KEN
          Hey, don't put this on me. You left
          your pill bottle out.

                    MALCOLM
          My pills!

Malcolm's eyes go wide.

INT. BATHROOM - NIGHT

Malcolm rushes in. His pill bottle is missing.

                    MALCOLM
          Where are my pills, Ken?

                    KEN
          Little bugger cleaned the bottle
          out.

                    MALCOLM
          No, no... You're kidding, you've
          got to be joking.

                    KEN
          I'm afraid not.

Malcolm sits on the toilet and rubs his temples.

                    KEN (CONT'D)
          Anyway, we're almost done here. I
          figured I would just come back by
          and drop Eisenhower off so you
          don't have to make an extra trip.

Malcolm nods his head.

                    MALCOLM
          See you soon.

INT. LIVING ROOM - LATER

Malcolm sits on his couch staring at the clock until he sees
a pair of headlights pull into his driveway. He gets up.

Ken enters with Eisenhower on a leash. Eisenhower wags his
tail and cheerfully barks at Malcolm. Malcolm gets down on
his knees to greet Eisenhower.

                    MALCOLM
          Hey, big guy, I'm so glad you're
          okay.

He stands back up.

                    MALCOLM (CONT'D)
          Sorry I yelled at you.

                    KEN
          It's okay. Sorry to rush things but
          it's late and I should get going.
          We'll have to talk about your
          meeting soon.

They shake hands.

                    MALCOLM
          Be careful, I think it's supposed
          to rain.

Ken opens the door to a heavy downpour.

                    KEN
          Yeah, I think you might be right.

                    MALCOLM
          In that closet to your right is an
          umbrella, you can have it.

INSERT - A STRANGER STANDS OUTSIDE WATCHING THEM

BACK TO SCENE

Ken opens the door and digs through the closet. He comes out
with an umbrella. He nods his head at Malcolm and exits the
trailer as he opens up the umbrella.

Malcolm turns to Eisenhower who is standing next to him.

                    MALCOLM
          You're in big trouble.

INT. TRAILER - BEDROOM - NIGHT

Malcolm lays in bed asleep. Eisenhower at the foot of the
bed, curled up.

A thumping sound comes from outside of the bedroom.
Eisenhower lifts his head.

The thumping continues.

The hairs on Eisenhower's back stand up.

Thump, thump...

Eisenhower snarls at the bedroom door. Malcolm wakes up.

Thump, thump...

Eisenhower jumps off the bed and exits the room to
investigate.

                    MALCOLM
          Who's there?

Eisenhower howls in pain.

                    MALCOLM (CONT'D)
          Eisenhower!

Malcolm opens a drawer in his night stand and pulls out a
flashlight. He shines it at the doorway.

Silence.

                    MALCOLM (CONT'D)
          I have a gun!

Thump, thump...

A long, drawn-out, moan comes from just outside his bedroom.
Malcolm shakily aims his flashlight at the door.
Heart racing.

Thump, thump...

Now the thumping sounds like it is coming from somewhere inside his room. He quickly shines the light around the room.

Suddenly, a grey, decrepit hand reaches from the ground and grabs his bed sheets.

Malcolm jumps back. He scrambles as he backs to the wall.

The hand slowly pulls itself up onto the bed. A decaying corpse covered in rotten burnt flesh emerges over the side of the bed.

Blood squirts out of holes in its body and black bile oozes from its mouth. Its eyes are yellow and bloodshot. Malcolm recognizes the corpse as Nelson.

> NELSON
> *You could've saved us...*

Malcolm holds out his hands to shield himself from the corpse.

> MALCOLM
> I never meant for you to die!

He kicks at Nelson's hand as he attempts to grab his leg.

> NELSON
> *You watched us die... You tried to*
> *forget about us...*

> MALCOLM
> I would never forget!

Nelson grabs Malcolm's leg and pulls him down. He wraps his hands around Malcolm's neck and squeezes tightly.

> NELSON
> *Join us... Before it's too late...*

Malcolm struggles to break free but Nelson is too strong.

> NELSON (CONT'D)
> *They will kill you...*

Malcolm grabs his flashlight and knocks Nelson in the head with it. The head pops off of its shoulders and falls to the ground.

The body sits upright for a moment. Malcolm looks over the side of his bed at the head. It turns around and growls at him. Then, the body throws itself on top of him.

INT. TRAILER - BEDROOM - DAY

Malcolm wakes with a start, panting. He examines the room.
Eisenhower is gone.

                    MALCOLM
          Eisenhower! Come here, boy!

Nothing.

INT. KITCHEN - DAY

Malcolm checks the clock.

                    MALCOLM
          If you don't come out, I'm going to
          eat without you!

He opens the pantry and pulls out dog food. He shakes it.

Still nothing.

                    MALCOLM (CONT'D)
          Last call for breakfast or you're
          starving!

He continues to walk around the trailer. A small pool of
water is on the floor.

INT. LIVING ROOM - DAY

He walks into the living room to find Eisenhower laying
stretched out on the floor.

                    MALCOLM
          There you are.

Eisenhower doesn't move.

Malcolm kneels down to Eisenhower and nudges him.

                    MALCOLM (CONT'D)
          Wake up. Time to eat.

Malcolm picks up his dog. Eisenhower is limp.

                    MALCOLM (CONT'D)
          No... No, please... No!

Malcolm cries as he hugs his dog's lifeless body.

EXT. MALCOLM'S YARD - DAY

Malcolm is holding a small box. He stands over a recently dug
hole in the ground. He carefully places the box in the hole.

He uses a shovel to burry the box. Once finished, Malcolm
kneels in front of the grave, eyes watery.

                    MALCOLM
          So long, friend.

He reaches places his hand on top of the grave.

INT. TRAILER - BATHROOM - DAY

Malcolm washes his hands. He looks at himself in the mirror.
He is a wreck, eyes red from crying, dark bags under his
eyes.

His reflection smirks back at him. Malcolm gawks, bewildered.
He opens the mirror. Nothing behind it except the medicine
cabinet.

He closes it again and his reflection speaks.

                    SHADOW MALCOLM
          Look at you, pathetic. I'm
          disgusted to share a conscious with
          you.

                    MALCOLM
          Y-you're not real.

Shadow Malcolm raises his hand in front of his face. Malcolm
uncontrollably matches his movements. His eyes dart from
Shadow Malcolm to his hand and back.

Then, Shadow Malcolm lifts his other hand. In this one he is
holding a straight razor, as is Malcolm. He slowly brings the
razor closer to his other hand.

Malcolm shakes his head.

                    MALCOLM (CONT'D)
          Please, no. Don't.

Shadow Malcolm slashes the palm of his hand, causing Malcolm
to do the same. He cries out in agony.

                    SHADOW MALCOLM
          Now that I have your attention.
          There are things happening that you
          don't understand.
                         (MORE)

                    SHADOW MALCOLM (CONT'D)
          If you want to live, you better
          listen to what I say.

Malcolm looks around as if to check if anyone is watching.

                    SHADOW MALCOLM (CONT'D)
          You're not who you think you are.

                    MALCOLM
          I don't know what you're talking
          about!

                    SHADOW MALCOLM
          There's a reason you keep having
          these visions, and it's not the
          pills.

                    MALCOLM
          Then what's causing them?

                    SHADOW MALCOLM
          The book. The yellow book. The
          answers are in the book.

                    MALCOLM
          You're not making sense.

Malcolm closes his eyes.

                    MALCOLM (CONT'D)
          This isn't real. This isn't real.

He opens his eyes. Shadow Malcolm has returned to being
nothing more than a reflection. Malcolm examines his cut up
hand.

INT. KITCHEN - LATER

Malcolm is sitting at the kitchen table. He is talking on the
phone. He nervously taps his fingers on the table as he
speaks.

                    MALCOLM
          It just seems like there's been so
          much going on around me lately...
          They're getting worse... I'll
          explain tonight...

Malcolm hangs up the phone. As he does, he notices a strange
marking on Eisenhower's food bowl. The marking is in blood
and looks like the number *'2'* in Roman Numerals.

INT. THERAPIST OFFICE - NIGHT

Malcolm enters, two cups of coffee in hand. He address the
Therapist who sits at his desk, reading from the yellow book.

                    MALCOLM
          They didn't have the creamer you
          wanted, I hope this works.

The Therapist looks up from his book, smiling.

                    THERAPIST
          Good evening, Mr. Tracey. Take a
          seat, I'll join you in a moment.
          Let me just find a stopping place.

Malcolm sits on the couch. He places the two cups of coffee
on the table next to it. The Therapist speaks to Malcolm
while he reads.

                    THERAPIST (CONT'D)
          On the phone you seemed pretty
          agitated. Did anything happen that
          I should know about?

                    MALCOLM
          Uh, well... The uh... The
          hallucinations have gotten worse. I
          only have nightmares lately and
          it's been hard to tell when I'm
          awake or asleep.

The Therapist looks up, eyebrows raised.

                    THERAPIST
          Have you been taking the medication
          I prescribed you?

                    MALCOLM
          Yeah, I think that's actually
          what's causing everything.

The Therapist sets his book down.

                    THERAPIST
          Tell me more about these
          hallucinations.

                    MALCOLM
          Well, they're mostly about my past.
          My time in the service. I keep
          seeing... The dead. It's almost as
          if they're calling to me.

                    THERAPIST
          So they speak to you. What do they
          say?

Malcolm thinks for a moment, then shakes his head.

                    MALCOLM
          It's not really anything important.

The Therapist narrows his eyes. He stands up and pats the
yellow book on his desk.

                    THERAPIST
          It just so happens that I was just
          reading about these side-effects in
          this book.

Malcolm's eyes light up.

                    MALCOLM
          That's the book!

                    THERAPIST
          Pardon?

                    MALCOLM
          I mean, that's the same book that
          the doctors had.

                    THERAPIST
          Ah, yes. How perceptive of you.
          This book contains extensive
          knowledge of the treatment you are
          going through.

                    MALCOLM
          Where can I get one of those books?

The Therapist chuckles.

                    THERAPIST
          Oh, this is not something for sale.
          Each of these books are hand-
          written by the doctors. Given to a
          select few of their trusted
          colleagues.

                    MALCOLM
          Is there any way I can look through
          it?

                    THERAPIST
          I'm sorry, but that wouldn't be
          possible. The information in here
          is not for patient's eyes.

The Therapist opens a drawer in his desk and places the book
in it.

                    THERAPIST (CONT'D)
          Now let's get back to you. Have you
          had any recent violent urges?

INT./EXT. MALCOLM'S CAR (MOVING) - NIGHT

It's raining outside, visibility low. Headlights from the car
behind Malcolm shine in his eyes.

                    MALCOLM
          Just go around me, asshole.

Lights flash on and a siren rings. It's a cop.

                    MALCOLM (CONT'D)
          You've got to be kidding me. One
          thing after another.

Malcolm pulls over and the squad car pulls behind him. He
sighs as he digs through his glove compartment for his
registration.

Once he has his license and registration he waits. The cop
car sits behind him, flashing lights still on.

He rolls down his window and pokes his head out. The driver's
door of the squad car is open but the officer is nowhere to
be seen.

Malcolm returns back inside his car. He jumps as he sees that
the OFFICER is standing directly in front of his car.

                    MALCOLM (CONT'D)
          Can I help you, Officer?

The Officer remains still. Malcolm holds up his license and
registration.

                    MALCOLM (CONT'D)
          I have my information.

The sound of the rain hitting the ground drowns out all other
sounds.

Malcolm rolls his eyes. He unlocks his car.

                    MALCOLM (CONT'D)
          I'm stepping out of the car. I'll
          keep my hands where you can see
          them.

Suddenly, the Officer jumps on the hood of Malcolm's car,
leaving a dent. Malcolm quickly locks his door. The Officer
gets on all fours and crawls on the roof of the car like a
spider.

Malcolm's eyes follow the sound of the Officer. Then, the
Officer reaches in through Malcolm's open window and grabs
his shirt.

Malcolm shifts his car into drive and slams his foot on the
pedal. The car begins to accelerate faster and faster.

The Officer drops down to look at Malcolm. However, it's not
the Officer. Instead, it is the soldier that Malcolm killed
in Germany.

The number *1* in Roman Numerals is written on his forehead
in blood. The soldier lets go of Malcolm and reaches for the
door handle.

Malcolm abruptly slams on his breaks, sending the soldier
flying off of the car into the darkness. He stays parked for
a moment, eyes wide, panting.

T.V. SCREEN -- DAY

The morning news broadcast plays. There is a MIDDLE-AGED MAN
on the screen sitting at a desk in the news studio talking to
the camera.

As he talks, a picture of a young male cop appears on the top
right-hand side of the screen.

                    NEWS BROADCASTER
          Just last night in Sherman Oaks, an
          officer was murdered in a hit-and-
          run accident. We've got news
          reporter Patrick Davis on location,
          Patrick.

The news cuts to a short, burly man in a sports jacket
holding a microphone.

                    PATRICK DAVIS
          Thank you, Tom. I am here in
          Sherman Oaks on Sun Ray Boulevard
          where 27 year old, Jason Streeble
          was struck by a car late last
          night. A driver passed by a little
          later and discovered the body on
          the side of the road and decided to
          pull over to check things out.
          Shortly after, they alerted
          authorities.

The news camera pans to the same cop car that pulled Malcolm
over.

                    PATRICK DAVIS (CONT'D)
          It was quickly determined that the
          squad car shown here belonged to
          Jason.

INT. TRAILER - LIVING ROOM - DAY

Malcolm is on the couch watching the news. He narrows his
eyes suspiciously.

EXT. DRIVEWAY - DAY

Malcolm examines the dent on the hood of his car. He notices
on his driver's door that the officer left a mark in blood
that resembles the number '3' in Roman Numerals.

INT. TRAILER - KITCHEN - DAY

Malcolm flips through his mail as he speaks on the phone.

                    MALCOLM
          ...Monday is fine, yeah.. Okay,
          thank you for getting me in... You
          too. Bye.

He lands on an envelope from the Pet Hospital.

Malcolm sits down at the kitchen table and opens the
envelope. Inside is a letter. His face drops in frustration
as he skims through it.

INT. CAR (MOVING) - DAY

Malcolm pulls up to a stop light. An OFFICER pulls up next to
him. He doesn't notice at first.

He glances over and sees the cop looking back. Malcolm begins to tap nervously on his steering wheel. The officer does not break his stare.

The officer lowers his sunglasses, squinting his eyes at the hood of Malcolm's car. As he does this, the light turns green and Malcolm takes off.

EXT./INT. THERAPIST OFFICE - DAY

Malcolm is at the door of the Therapist's Office. A sign on the door reads: *"OUT TO LUNCH"* and it shows a time of *"1:00pm"*.

He checks his watch, hesitates for a moment, then turns back towards his car.

Clenching his fists, he makes a split-second decision and tries the door. He pulls it, it's unlocked.

Malcolm scans the office when he enters. The Therapist is gone. He rushes over to the desk and begins digging through the drawers.

The first drawer he opens contains dozens of boxes of raisins. The next drawer contains maps stacked with circles over various locations, some of which are crossed off.

Finally, Malcolm opens a drawer to reveal the yellow leather-bound book. He takes it out and closes the drawer. He sets the book on the desk and opens it. He skims through the pages.

He stops on a page with a picture of the Aztec Sun God, labeled *"Huitzilopochtli"*. On that page, he reads a few sentences:

"...every ten years the Bright One will shine his light down on Earth and choose a new vessel. The subject will be prepared for the arrival of the Bright One's spawn..."

Malcolm flips through some more pages. He finds a page that his own picture is tucked into.

"Subject must kill to survive." and *"Must return to the Trigger Sight for assimilation."* He looks up, scans the room, then back down.

As Malcolm reads, he notices something; sitting on the Therapist's desk is a framed picture. He picks it up to get a better look.

The picture is of the Therapist back when he was about
Malcolm's age surrounded by the doctors from the gathering.
However, the doctors all appear to be the same age as when he
met them.

Suddenly, the bell dings that signals someone has entered the
office. Malcolm's head shoots up to see that the Therapist
has walked in.

He sneakily sets the picture down and rips the page with his
picture out of the book and closes it. He hides the page
behind his back. When the Therapist notices Malcolm, he
addresses him.

                    THERAPIST
          Malcolm, what a pleasant surprise.
          I guess you didn't see my note on
          the door.

                    MALCOLM
          Oh, hello... I did actually, but I
          needed to speak with you.

Malcolm sneakily slides the page into his back pocket.

                    THERAPIST
          Oh?

                    MALCOLM
          I- I'm actually going to be out of
          town for a while and wanted to let
          you know ahead of time.

The Therapist nods his head.

                    THERAPIST
          Oh, right. Germany.

Malcolm narrows his eyes.

                    MALCOLM
          I don't think I mentioned that to
          you.

                    THERAPIST
          You must've. How else would I have
          known?

                    MALCOLM
          I suppose...

The Therapist claps his hands together.

                    THERAPIST
          While you're here, can I get you
          something to drink?

                    MALCOLM
          No, I'm okay, I should get going.

Malcolm heads for the door. The Therapist extends his hand
out.

                    THERAPIST
          Thank you for stopping by!

Malcolm walks past the Therapist without shaking his hand.
The Therapist watches him leave and notices the paper in his
back pocket. He then walks over to his desk.

He picks up the yellow book, noticing Malcolm went through
it. He smirks.

INT. MAKEUP ROOM - DAY

A MAKEUP ARTIST is applying makeup to Malcolm's face. He sits
still in front of a mirror. The Makeup Artist opens a
container, it's empty.

                    MAKEUP ARTIST
          Shoot, I'll be right back.

Malcolm nods and the Makeup Artist leaves the room. He
continues to stare straight ahead. Shadow Malcolm appears in
his reflection.

                    SHADOW MALCOLM
          Hey, Pretty Boy.

                    MALCOLM
          Not again. Please, leave me alone.
          I can't keep doing this!

                    SHADOW MALCOLM
          You and me, we're one in the same.
          You'll never be alone. Now listen
          carefully. We need to do something
          about Ida. She wants to see you
          fail. She thinks she's better than
          you.

                    MALCOLM
          That's not true.

                    SHADOW MALCOLM
          You know it's true! I'm on your
          side, can't you see?

                    MALCOLM
          No you're not. You're evil.

                    SHADOW MALCOLM
          I'm necessary! It's the world
          that's evil. I'm here to help take
          care of your adversaries. We need
          to get rid of Ida.

                    MALCOLM
          And how do you plan to do that?

A devilish grin splits Shadow Malcolm's face. His teeth gleam
in the light.

                    MALCOLM (CONT'D)
          What? No... W-we can't do that.

                    SHADOW MALCOLM
          You don't have to do anything, I
          will take care of her for you.

                    MALCOLM
          We share a body, anything you do is
          going to affect both of us.

                    SHADOW MALCOLM
          I didn't realize that I was sharing
          a body with such a coward.

                    MALCOLM
          We're not going to kill her!

                    SHADOW MALCOLM
          Suit yourself.

Shadow Malcolm returns to being nothing more than Malcolm's
reflection. The Makeup Artists re-enters the room holding a
new container.

                    MAKEUP ARTIST
          Now this should be more than
          enough.

INT. FILM SET - MILITARY BASE - DAY

Malcolm and Ida are dressed in military attire. They are
huddled around Quentin as he speaks to them.

                    QUENTIN
          Okay, so here's the lay down: you
          both just found out you're getting
          shipped to Germany but the other
          one doesn't know; Malcolm to join
          the front lines, and Ida to preside
          over intelligence. You have a
          hidden love for each other but
          neither will admit it. This scene
          is all about subtext. You're saying
          goodbye without saying it, you're
          expressing your love for one
          another without expressing it. For
          all your character's know, this is
          the last time you will see each
          other.

Quentin slowly backs away.

                    QUENTIN (CONT'D)
          And ACTION.

Caked in makeup, Malcolm still has massive bags under his
eyes. Ida fixes his collar

                    IDA
          I don't know what you would do
          without me, soldier.

As Ida finishes fixing the collar she smiles. Eyes watery.

                    MALCOLM
          I sure hope that I never have to
          find out.

Ida pats Malcolm's chest. The two look into each other's
eyes.

                    IDA
          What are your plans for after the
          war?

Malcolm takes a moment to think.

                    MALCOLM
          I haven't put much thought into it.

                    IDA
          I know what I'm going to do.

                    MALCOLM
          What's that?

                    IDA
          I'm going to dance. Ballroom gown,
          fancy food, the works.

                    MALCOLM
          That's not something I'd expect to
          hear from you.

                    IDA
          I've spent so much time trying to
          be something I'm not. I think it's
          about time I start trying to be
          myself.

                    MALCOLM
          That sounds nice.

                    IDA
          It would be nicer to have someone
          to dance with.

                    MALCOLM
          Wish I knew how to dance.

                    IDA
          It's not something you learn. It's
          something you feel. You need to let
          the music take over you.

                    MALCOLM
          I suppose you're right.

                    IDA
          I suppose so.

Ida takes a step forward. The world around them begins to
disappear into darkness.

Then, Ida's eyes roll into the back of her head and her skin
turns blue. She reaches out to Malcolm and speaks in a deep
sinister voice.

                    IDA (CONT'D)
          Join us, Malcolm. Join us before
          it's too late.

Malcolm stands frozen in horror. He shakes his head.

                    MALCOLM
          No, I'm not ready... I'm not ready!

Ida frowns in frustration.

                    IDA
          What are you talking about?

Quentin flips through the script for the film, confused.

                    DIRECTOR
          Cut!

                    IDA
               (To Malcolm)
          What is your deal? Are you
          purposefully sabotaging this film?

Quentin walks over to the two.

                    DIRECTOR
          Everything okay?

Ida storms off set. Malcolm finally comes to.

                    MALCOLM
          I'm sorry, I don't know what's
          going on.

Quentin puts his arm around Malcolm's shoulder and walks him
off set.

                    QUENTIN
          Listen, I totally get it. Coming
          from commercials to a big movie set
          can be intimidating. Just take all
          your inhibitions and throw them
          out. Do it with me, come on.

Quentin grabs the air and pretends to throw it in an
imaginary trash can.

Malcolm half-heartedly follows along.

                    QUENTIN (CONT'D)
          Perfect. You know what I do when I
          get like this?

                    MALCOLM
          Throw away your inhibitions?

                    QUENTIN
          No. We've already covered that.

Quentin makes sure nobody is watching. He pulls a flask out
of his back pocket.

                    QUENTIN (CONT'D)
          Here. A little liquid courage to
          get you through the rest of the
          day.

Malcolm leans in.

                    MALCOLM
          Are you sure?

Quentin eggs him on.

                    QUENTIN
          Go ahead.

Malcolm grabs the flask and takes a swig. Quentin pats him on
the back.

                    QUENTIN (CONT'D)
          Just think, next week we'll be in
          another country and today will be a
          distant memory. Now let's film a
          movie!

INT. TRAILER - BATHROOM - DAY

Malcolm flips the light on. He speaks to the mirror.

                    MALCOLM
          Come out, I know you're there.

Nothing.

                    MALCOLM (CONT'D)
          Listen to me!

Still nothing.

Nostrils flaring, he punches the mirror, shattering it.
Shards of glass fall to the ground and Malcolm is left
staring at a broken image of himself.

INT. KITCHEN - DAY

Malcolm is at the table, arms crossed. The room is silent
aside from the ticking clock. Un-prompted, he starts to laugh
uncontrollably. As he laughs, tears fall down his face.

His hysterical episode is halted by a knock at the door.
Without moving a muscle, Malcolm calls out.

                    MALCOLM
          Come in!

The door creaks open and footsteps approach. Malcolm clenches
his fist.

Ken enters the kitchen and sits across the table from
Malcolm.

                    KEN
          You look like hell.

Malcolm releases the tension in his hand.

                    MALCOLM
          Feel it, too.

                    KEN
          I came as quickly as I could. All
          I'm saying, still no raise.

                    MALCOLM
          I didn't know who else to go to,
          they would all think I'm crazy.

As Malcolm speaks, his eyes dart from Ken to his front door
and back.

                    KEN
          Go on.

                    MALCOLM
          I'm not quite sure what it is, to
          be honest... Lately there have just
          been so many coincidences...

                    KEN
          I know what you mean. I think I
          read somewhere that it means that
          we're about to have a bad
          earthquake.

                    MALCOLM
          No, not like that. There have just
          been things that have happened that
          I can't quite explain.

                    KEN
          Yes, that is the definition of a
          coincidence.

                    MALCOLM
          I need to you take me seriously.
          Some crazy shit has been happening
          and I think it has to do with the
          doctors.

                    KEN
          You're still on about that?

                    MALCOLM
          Well ever since then, and even
          before then I have been having
          these visions.

                    KEN
          You mean, like your PTSD?

Malcolm shakes his head.

                    MALCOLM
          I don't think so. This is
          different.

                    KEN
          I'm not sure if I understand.

                    MALCOLM
          Well when I met with the doctors,
          they had this yellow book.

                    KEN
          Okay...

                    MALCOLM
          Well, I managed to get my hands on
          one of the books and it went on
          about the Aztec Sun God and
          sacrifices for immortality...

Ken is taken aback.

                    KEN
          W-what?

                    MALCOLM
          That's what I'm saying! I think
          this is all somehow connected to
          me.

                    KEN
          What makes you think that?

Malcolm takes out the page he stole from the book and sets it
in front of Ken. Ken examines it.

                    MALCOLM
          That's not even all of it.

Ken sets the page back down on the table.

                    MALCOLM (CONT'D)
          I got a letter back from the vet.
          They told me my medication was a
          placebo.

                    KEN
          I'm sorry, I'm not up to date on my
          medical terms.

                    MALCOLM
          Sugar pills, fakes. They're not
          real.

                    KEN
          But that doesn't make sense.

                    MALCOLM
          Exactly! There's something going on
          and we need to get to the bottom of
          it. When I met with the doctors,
          they kept talking about a *Process*.
          I don't know what's happening but I
          feel like my life is in danger.

                    KEN
          We can't let them get away with
          this. Something needs to be done!

                    MALCOLM
          So you believe me?

                    KEN
          I'm paid to believe you! But also,
          I'm your friend. So it's kind of
          required.

                    MALCOLM
          Oh, thank God. So what do you think
          we should do?

                    KEN
          Remind me, where did you meet with
          these doctors?

INT. KEN'S CAR - DAY

Ken parks in a spot for the community center.

INT. COMMUNITY CENTER - HALLWAY - DAY

He walks down the hall to the conference room. He cups his
hands and looks in through the window in the door.

The room is completely empty. A bulletin board with the
conference room schedule is on the wall next to the door. The
monthly meeting with the doctors is not listed.

EXT. KEN'S CAR (MOVING) - COMMUNITY CENTER - DAY

Ken pulls out of the parking lot. Dr. Hernandez is in a
parked car in the same lot. He follows Ken.

INT. PHONE BOOTH - EMPTY ROAD - DAY

Ken is on the phone. He speaks a mile a minute.

                    KEN
          Malcolm, I stopped by the Community
          Center. Nothing's there. The
          meeting wasn't even listed on the
          schedule.

He pauses for a moment, as if he heard something.

                    KEN (CONT'D)
          I'm going to call the authorities.

He hangs up and dials for the operator. The phone rings.

                    OPERATOR
          Operator.

                    KEN
          I need to be connected to the Los
          Angeles Dispatch center.

                    OPERATOR
          Thank you.

Phone static. Then, a crackling noise. Ken taps his foot as
he waits.

                    EMERGENCY DISPATCHER
          L.A. Dispatch, what's your
          emergency?

                    KEN
          Hello, this is Ken Ryan and there
          is-

Ken is cut off by a dial tone. He checks the phone. He enters the number again. Dial tone. He slams the phone against the wall of the phone booth.

                    KEN (CONT'D)
          Piece of shit!

Then Dr. Hernandez's car drives slowly by and stops on the side of the road. Ken quickly exits the phone booth and heads straight for his car.

As he gets back to his vehicle he sees Dr. Hernandez holding a blunt object in the reflection of his car.

INT. TRAILER - KITCHEN - NIGHT

Malcolm stands with the phone in his hand, it's ringing. No answer. He hangs up and sits down at the table. He rests his head in his hands.

The phone rings. Malcolm's head shoots up. He rushes over and answers it.

                    MALCOLM
          Ken!

                    MYSTERIOUS VOICE
          You shouldn't have brought him into
          this.

                    MALCOLM
          Who's this?

The call ends. Malcolm stands frozen in place listening to the dial tone.

INT. BEDROOM - NIGHT

Malcolm is on the floor. The box from his closet lays open in front of him. On the ground next to the box are his uniform, Chief's canteen, and the combat knife.

He sets the canteen and uniform back in the box. He picks up the knife and stares at his reflection in the blade.

INT. AIRPLANE CABIN - NIGHT

Malcolm is sitting next to Ida. She is sleeping and their overhead light is off. He uses a small flashlight to examine the page of the book he tore out.

THE PLANE LANDS -- DAY

INT. AIRPORT - DAY

Malcolm and Ida are waiting at luggage return. As they wait,
Quentin comes over to them.

                    QUENTIN
          So I have some bad news. There was
          a mix up at the hotel and Ida's
          room was apparently never booked.

                    IDA
          They didn't assign my room?

                    QUENTIN
          I'm afraid not. I was thinking
          since Malcolm has a two person
          bedroom he might be able to let you
          stay with him during our time here.
          Would that be okay? I know this is
          last minute but we just found out
          about this situation.

                    IDA
          There's no other options?

                    QUENTIN
          Not at this point, unfortunately.
               (To Malcolm)
          Is this okay with you?

                    MALCOLM
          I mean, if there's nothing else
          that can be done...

Quentin smiles and grabs Malcolm's shoulder. He gives it a
little shake.

                    QUENTIN
          Good man. I knew I could count on
          you.

INT. HOTEL ROOM - DAY

The door opens and Malcolm and Ida walk in with their
suitcases. Ida stops in her tracks. There is only one king-
size bed in the center of the room.

                    IDA
          I thought they said it was a two
          person bedroom.

                    MALCOLM
          Guess when they said two person
          they meant for a couple.

                    IDA
          Oh, we are not doing this.

Ida walks over to the bed and removes the pillows. She uses
them to set up a wall between the two halves of the bed.

                    MALCOLM
          What are you doing?

                    IDA
          Making sure that you stay on your
          side of the bed.

Malcolm laughs.

                    MALCOLM
          I don't think that'll be a problem.

LATER

The lights are off. Malcolm and Ida are in bed, on their
respective sides. Malcolm is using his flashlight to look
over a map of Germany. He marks a location: *"Trigger Sight"*.

Ida is wearing a sleep mask. She takes it off and addresses
Malcolm.

                    IDA
          Can you give it a rest already?

Malcolm looks up from his map.

                    MALCOLM
          Just a second.

                    IDA
          I'm exhausted. I just want to go to
          sleep.

                    MALCOLM
          Okay.

Malcolm places the map in his suitcase. The light from his
flashlight reflects off of the combat knife. He tucks it into
his bag and turns off the flashlight.

Ida immediately begins to snore. Malcolm lays back in bed and
pulls the covers over him. He stares up at the ceiling.

After a few moments, a flickering light reflects off of the
ceiling. Then, smoke begins to fill the room. The sound of a
crackling fire comes from the foot of the bed.

Malcolm quickly sits upright.

Silence.

The fire is gone and the room is dark. Standing motionless in
the corner of the room is what looks like a man draped in
white robes. Malcolm squints his eyes to get a better look.

Nearly paralyzed with fear, he reaches down into his suitcase
and pulls out the flashlight. He shines it in the figure's
direction.

Nothing.

Ida shuffles on her side of the bed.

                    IDA
          For the love of God. Turn that damn
          light off.

                    MALCOLM
          Sorry, had to go to the bathroom.

Ida turns away from Malcolm. He clicks the light off.

INT. HOTEL - LOBBY - DAY

Quentin is holding a cup of coffee. He smiles at Malcolm and
Ida who walk over to him.

                    QUENTIN
          I hope you guys slept well. We've
          got a full day ahead of us.

Ida is all smiles. Malcolm has bags under his eyes.

                    IDA
          I actually got some of the best
          sleep I've had in months.

                    QUENTIN
          That's great!

MONTAGE:

EXT. BERLIN - DAY

Malcolm fights alongside his fellow soldiers outside of the
city.

INT. U.S. BASE - DAY

Ida is going over a map of the country. She marks spots that
Malcolm's men have breached.

INTER-CUT

-Malcolm's men are now in an alley in the city. They cut off
German soldiers walking by and pull them into the alley.

-A folder is thrown in front of Ida labeled *"OPERATION:
STOLPEN VON INNEN"*.

Ida opens the folder. Inside are pictures of the squad of men
involved in the operation. She flips through the pictures and
lands on one of Malcolm. In shock, she drops the folder.

-Malcolm and one of the other men in his squad are dressed in
German uniforms. He takes off his helmet and pulls out a
picture of Ida.

-Ida puts on a gown.

-Malcolm puts on boots.

-Ida pulls up her pantyhose.

-Malcolm loads a gun.

-Ida applies lipstick. She grabs a gun off her dresser and
places it in her purse.

EXT. BRANDENBURG GATE - NIGHT

The lights and cameras are set up. Quentin brings Malcolm and
Ida in for a talk.

                    QUENTIN
          This is the big emotional moment of
          the film. Malcolm, your character
          is about to go on his suicide
          mission to end the war against
          Germany, unknowing that Ida's
          character is on her way to you to
          confess her love.
                    (MORE)

                    QUENTIN (CONT'D)
          This reunion is significant because
          Malcolm's character has already
          accepted his fate but when Ida's
          character expresses her love he
          must make the ultimate decision.

Quentin pats them both on the back and smiles.

                    QUENTIN (CONT'D)
          You've got this.

The U.S. soldiers are undercover in German uniforms. They
sneak through the Brandenburg Gate. When they get to the
center, Ida calls from behind them.

                    IDA
             Thompson!

They stop in their tracks.

                    MALCOLM
             Valerie?

Ida rushes over to meet them. The other soldiers stand guard
while they talk.

                    MALCOLM (CONT'D)
          What are you doing here?

Malcolm embraces Ida, she is crying.

                    IDA
          I can't let you do this.

                    MALCOLM
          You can't be here, it's too
          dangerous for Americans.

                    IDA
          I won't leave you.

                    MALCOLM
          But you have to. I don't want you
          to get hurt.

Ida opens her mouth, hesitates for a moment.

                    IDA
          I love you.

Malcolm stares at her in disbelief.

                    MALCOLM
          I-I love you too.

The two lean in and kiss. A few seconds pass by.

                    QUENTIN
          And, cut!

Quentin smiles as he holds two thumbs up.

                    QUENTIN (CONT'D)
          Excellent!

They continue kissing.

                    QUENTIN (CONT'D)
          Cut!

It's no use. The other actors awkwardly avert their eyes.

                    QUENTIN (CONT'D)
          Alright guys, good job.

INT. HOTEL ROOM - NIGHT

The door flies open and Malcolm and Ida stumble in, still
kissing. They make their way to the bed. Malcolm shoves Ida
onto it and she grabs his shirt and rips it off.

They both quickly strip naked. Ida grabs Malcolm and pulls
him on the bed and jumps on top of him.

As Ida thrusts, Malcolm slowly brings his hand up to her neck
and gently begins to choke her.

Suddenly, the color drains from Malcolm's eyes and they begin
to glow. He tightens his grip around Ida's neck, wearing a
malicious grin. Shadow Malcolm is in control.

                    IDA
               (Panting)
          Too much.

Malcolm squeezes tighter.

                    IDA (CONT'D)
          Stop, you're hurting me.

Malcolm stands up, lifting Ida off the bed by her throat. She
gasps for air as she kicks her dangling feet at him.

Ida punches his arms but it's no use. Malcolm brings his
other hand up to her head and in one quick motion he snaps
her neck.

Her body goes limp. He drops her to the floor and she
crumples like paper.

Malcolm steps down from the bed, smirking. Grey eyes glowing
in the dark. The clock reads: *"11:11"*. Sitting next to the
clock is the map of Germany. He lowers his gaze to the combat
knife in his bag.

INT. HALLWAY - LATER

A HOUSEKEEPER wheels her cart of cleaning supplies down the
hall. She stops at Malcolm's room.

At the end of the hall an exit door blows open and close. She
sighs and walks over to the door and shuts it. Once she
returns to her cart she knocks on the door.

                    HOUSEKEEPER
          Housekeeping.

No answer. She opens the door and steps inside. As soon as
she enters, she screams.

INT. HOTEL ROOM - NIGHT

The horrified housekeeper is backed up against the wall.

She stands frozen in fear, gaping. Ida's corpse is propped up
by a lamp post that impales her body from the bottom of her
torso up through her neck.

Over the light is Ida's disemboweled head. The light shines
through her eyes and mouth holes. Above Ida's dead body, the
number *'4'* in Roman Numerals is painted in blood on the wall.

EXT. WILDERNESS - NIGHT

Malcolm stands before the bunker, naked. He is covered in
blood, knife in hand.

INT. GERMAN BUNKER - NIGHT

Malcolm slowly walks down the stairs.

The door is closed at the bottom of the stairs. A flickering
light shines through the gap under the door. He opens it and
steps into the sleeping quarters.

He slowly walks through the room. At the end of the room, the
metal door lays open. He continues through the doorway.

It is a spacious room lit by candlelight. The rug from the
conference room lays on the floor. Along the walls are
tapestries of the different stages of The Process.

In the center of the room is a concrete slab. Standing along
the walls are the doctors accompanied by others. They are all
draped in white cloaks.

Malcolm silently scans the room, looking at the tapestries.

The first depicts Spanish Conquistadors raiding the Aztec
empire, followed by the same men discovering the healing
power of the Sun. The men depicted in these ancient
tapestries look exactly like the doctors.

Another tapestry is of a man being fed Sunlight. The next
shows a man surrounded by an aura of light. After that, the
same man is tied up on a slab and is being burnt alive.

The last two tapestries depict the Conquistadors feasting on
the man's corpse and then in turn being surrounded by the
same aura.

Suddenly, one of the doctors closes the door behind Malcolm.
Dr. Hernandez steps forward.

                    DR. HERNANDEZ
          Brothers and sisters, after ten
          years of preparation, the subject
          has returned as it is written!

                    DOCTORS
          Hail the Process!

                    DR. HERNANDEZ
          The moment has come, the Process
          will finally be complete.

                    DOCTORS
          Hail the Process!

The doctors all begin to slowly surround Malcolm. He looks
down at his knife, the doctors are getting closer...

In one quick move he slits his own throat. The doctors scream
in terror as Malcolm falls to the floor, blood trickling from
his neck.

BLACK.

                    THERAPIST
          Malcolm. That's right, wake up.

INT. GERMAN BUNKER - LATER

Malcolm slowly opens his eyes. Above him is a small vent in
the ceiling that he can see the morning sky through. A bird
flies overhead.

The doctors stand around him in their white robes holding
their yellow books. He tries to sit up, he's tied to the
slab.

Laying on the slab around him are a pile of sticks that make
it look as though he is in a bird's nest.

His neck is wrapped in a bandage. His face fills with horror
as he struggles to break free of his restraints.

                    MALCOLM
          What's going on?

His voice is hoarse.

                    THERAPIST
          It's okay, Malcolm. This is all
          part of The Process.

                    MALCOLM
          Let me go! Let me out of here! Who
          the fuck are you people?

Malcolm struggles some more. It's no use. In the crowd of
cloaked figures, he notices a familiar face.

                    MALCOLM (CONT'D)
          Mia?

A little color comes back into his eyes. Next to her is the
man she left him for. She does not respond.

                    THERAPIST
          That's right.
               (Gesturing the man)
          Our brother Darius brought Mia into
          our organization early on in their
          relationship. Said he was tired of
          living on without someone to share
          in his eternity. We weren't going
          to accept her, however she had
          something to offer us.

                    MALCOLM
          Katherine...
               (To Mia)
          She loved you! She trusted you!

The Therapist hushes Malcolm. He nods to Dr. Silvia who then
wraps a cloth over Malcolm's mouth. Malcolm screams as he
does this.

                    THERAPIST
          I'm sorry, Malcolm, but it's time
          we finish The Process.

Mia and Darius take a step back.

Dr. Torres mixes blood with a pestle and mortar. Once he is
finished he sets it down on the slab next to Malcolm who is
still struggling.

Dr. Hernandez dips his index finger into the blood and slowly
raises it up for Malcolm to see. He then marks Malcolm's
forehead with one vertical line.

As he does this, Malcolm bends and contorts his body.

                    DR. HERNANDEZ
          One for the blood of the innocent
          shed for The Process.

EISENHOWER

The doctors all knock on their books.

He marks Malcolm's forehead again.

                    DR. HERNANDEZ
          Two for the blood of the ally shed
          for The Process.

THE OFFICER

The doctors once again knock on their books.

He marks Malcolm's forehead.

                    DR. HERNANDEZ
          Three for the blood of the enemy
          shed for The Process.

THE NAZI

The doctors knock.

He marks Malcolm's forehead one last time. As he does this, a
light shines down from the vent onto Malcolm. All color
leaves his eyes.

                    DR. HERNANDEZ
          Finally, four for the blood of the
          lover shed for The Process.

IDA

The doctors knock on their books. Dr. Hernandez licks the
blood off his finger. The Therapist hands Dr. Hernandez an
oil can.

                    DR. HERNANDEZ
          We reject the Bright One and shall
          consume his spawn to complete The
          Process and obtain his powers of
          immortality.

The doctors knock on their books. Dr. Hernandez pours the oil
on Malcolm.

                    DR. HERNANDEZ (CONT'D)
          We shall gain the years of the
          lives taken for the sake of The
          Process. All hail The Process!

                    DOCTORS
          All hail The Process! All hail The
          Process! All hail The Process!

Dr. Torres lights the fire and Malcolm begins to burn, the
smoke travels up through the vent. Malcolm struggles to break
free in vain.

The doctors knock on their books as he burns. Standing among
the doctors are apparitions of Nelson, Chief, and Ida.

Malcolm screams out in pain but there is no one to rescue
him. It's over.

Mia stands motionless, a single tear runs down her cheek.

The doctors continue to chant, they've completed The Process.

FADE OUT.

                    THE END